I Love Me!

For Kendel and Maya

WRITTEN BY: KIM DULANEY
ILLUSTRATED BY: SHERMAN BECK

I Love Me!

Published by
Unique Expressions, Inc.
P.O. Box 11869
Chicago, Illinois 60611
e-mail: readme4000@aol.com
1-888-README4
Printed By

317-329-9974
Fax 317-216-7148
6212 La Pas Trail
Indianapolis, IN 46268

ISBN 1-891636-02-2
Printed in The United States of America

I Love Me!

I love me...
just because I'm me.
There's no other person
I'd rather be.

I love my thick-curly-
coarse hair,
I even love these
old clothes I wear.

I love my lips and my nose
and yes, I love
my crusty old toes.

I look in the mirror with my beautiful eyes, and always happen to see my good side.

**Looking at the front,
side or back
I just can't find
anything I lack.**

I'm absolutely beautiful,
inside and out,
created by a perfectionist,
no doubt.

I know you feel the same
about you
because GOD made
you perfect too!!!!!!

I
Love
Me